This book belongs to:

Paige M. 2887
JA

AUTUMN
PUBLISHING

Written by Suzanne Fossey
Illustrated by Gina Maldonado
Designed by Lee Italiano
Edited by Suzanne Fossey

Copyright © 2019 Igloo Books Ltd

An imprint of Igloo Books Group,
part of Bonnier Books UK
bonnierbooks.co.uk

Published in 2019
by Igloo Books Ltd, Cottage Farm
Sywell, NN6 0BJ
All rights reserved, including the right of reproduction
in whole or in part in any form.

Manufactured in China. 1219 001
10 9 8 7 6 5 4 3 2 1

Library of Congress Cataloging-in-Publication
Data is available upon request.

ISBN 978-1-83852-398-5
autumnpublishing.co.uk
bonnierbooks.co.uk

Little
CHICK

AUTUMN
PUBLISHING

I started in a cozy egg, all snug and warm within.

I tapped and pecked and made a hole. The light came shining in.

At last, the eggshell cracked in two. I wiggled my way free.
"Hello there, my Little Chick!"
my mommy said to me.

"You must be hungry," Daddy said.
"We'll bring you food to eat."
He came back with a wiggly worm.
Oh, what a lovely treat!

Day by day I grew, till I was **big** enough to **fly.**
I felt scared. I was **so** small and we **were very high.**

"**Help,**" I cried.
"I'm falling!"

"Just flap your wings,"
said Dad.

I tried it, and I soared up!
I felt so very glad.

My feathers touched the **tops** of trees as I **flew** across the sky.

Everything looks **very** tiny when you're flying **up** so **high**.

Not long after,
Mommy said, "The leaves
have begun to fall.
We're going on a journey,
now that you're no
longer small."

"We're flying somewhere warm for winter. It's really for the best.

"So shake your tail and flap your wings. It's time to leave the nest."

We joined a hundred
other birds and soared
across the sea.

For miles and miles
we flew and flew,
far from our cozy tree.

The city was too **noisy** . . .

. . . and the **forest** was too **still**.

"But this waterfall is perfect!"
I chirruped with a trill.

For months we **stayed** down in
the **south**, till I was fully **grown**.
Then **springtime** came around again.
It was time to **fly** back **home**.

Along the way, I met a friend.
We made a lovely pair!

We built a nest
together, a home
for us to share.

It wasn't long before I laid
five eggs, all smooth and round.
I kept them warm and snuggly,
high above the ground.

One day, I heard some noises: little cracks and cricks. My eggs were hatching! And out came five fluffy, little...

... chicks!

Bluebird chicks hatch
from their eggs in spring.
They stay in the nest and their
parents bring them food until they learn
to fly. When fall comes, bluebirds fly south
to warmer places with hundreds of other birds, in
a journey called migration. They spend the winter
safe from cold weather and fly back north in
the spring to build their nests. The female
bluebirds lay eggs and keep them
warm by sitting on them until
they are ready to hatch.